• *Cavoy, Cavah, Cavoo!* •

BENEATH THE REEF

Say by Cal Devney

Illustrated by Olko Vladi

A Coding and Augmented Reality Book

Cavoy, Cavah, Cavoo!
Copyright © 2023 by Cal Devney
Augmented Reality (AR) animations by monkey3media

The Augmented Reality (AR) experiences that accompany this book rely on third party applications that are outside the control of the author, Blue Sea Books and monkey3media.

All rights reserved. No part of this publication may be reproduced, distributed, or transmitted in any form or by any means, including photocopying, recording, or other electronic or mechanical methods, without the prior written permission of the author, except in the case of brief quotations embodied in critical reviews and certain other non-commercial uses permitted by copyright law.

Tellwell Talent
www.tellwell.ca

ISBN
978-0-2288-8480-4 (Paperback)

Other books by Cal Devney

The Ick Erros
The Smoo Room
The Jungah

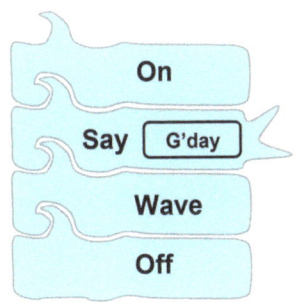

EXPERIENCE THIS IN AR

SCAN QR CODE > POINT PHONE AT PAGE > DISCOVER EXPERIENCE

On
Dig 3
Pause 5
Dig 3
Pause 5
Off

Two birds dug a hole in the soft white sand.
SWISH! The sand flew off their shovels
and over their shoulders.
Zoom and Stephen would dig until they found treasure.
They were searching for a chest full
of beautiful black opals.

CLINK! Something broke beneath Stephen's shell shovel.
Zoom leaned over a deep black hole that had appeared.
'Stephen, do you think something is
down there?' Zoom asked.
Oops! Zoom leaned too far and fell in.
Stephen leaned over to call after Zoom. 'Noooo . . . Zoom!'
Oops! Stephen leaned too far and fell in.

Zoom and Stephen landed on their feathery behinds.
Where were they?
They looked around, confused.
They were in a large cave, and they
could see colourful glowing lights.

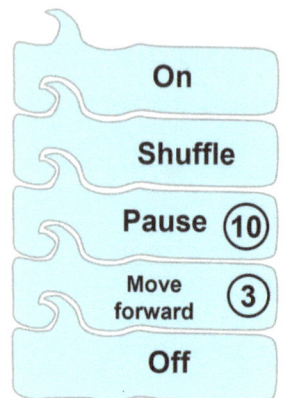

The lights were the leaves of plants that glowed in the colours of the rainbow.
The leaves twinkled like bright stars in the night sky.
There was a noise behind Zoom and Stephen.

The Trix Kix came out from behind the log where they had been hiding. The little Trix Kix marched like soldier crabs and looked like caterpillars. The Ick Erros came out from behind the rock where they had been hiding. The medium-sized Ick Erros hopped like kangaroos and looked like jellyfish.

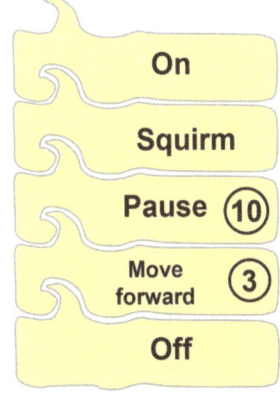

Zoom and Stephen watched the strange creatures.
The Trix Kix marched, and the Ick Erros
hopped towards Zoom and Stephen.
Zoom waved his wing and Stephen
smiled his biggest smile.
The Trix Kix waved back and said, 'G'day!'
The Ick Erros smiled back and said, 'Let's be mates!'
'Great plan, fair dinkum,' Zoom answered.
'We agree, too right,' Stephen answered.

An alarm call rang out, 'Eep! Eep!'
'EEP! EEP!'
Zoom and Stephen looked left and right,
up and down, their eyes wide.
The Trix Kix said, 'Oh my! Oh no!'
The Ick Erros said, 'The Bognicks are coming!'

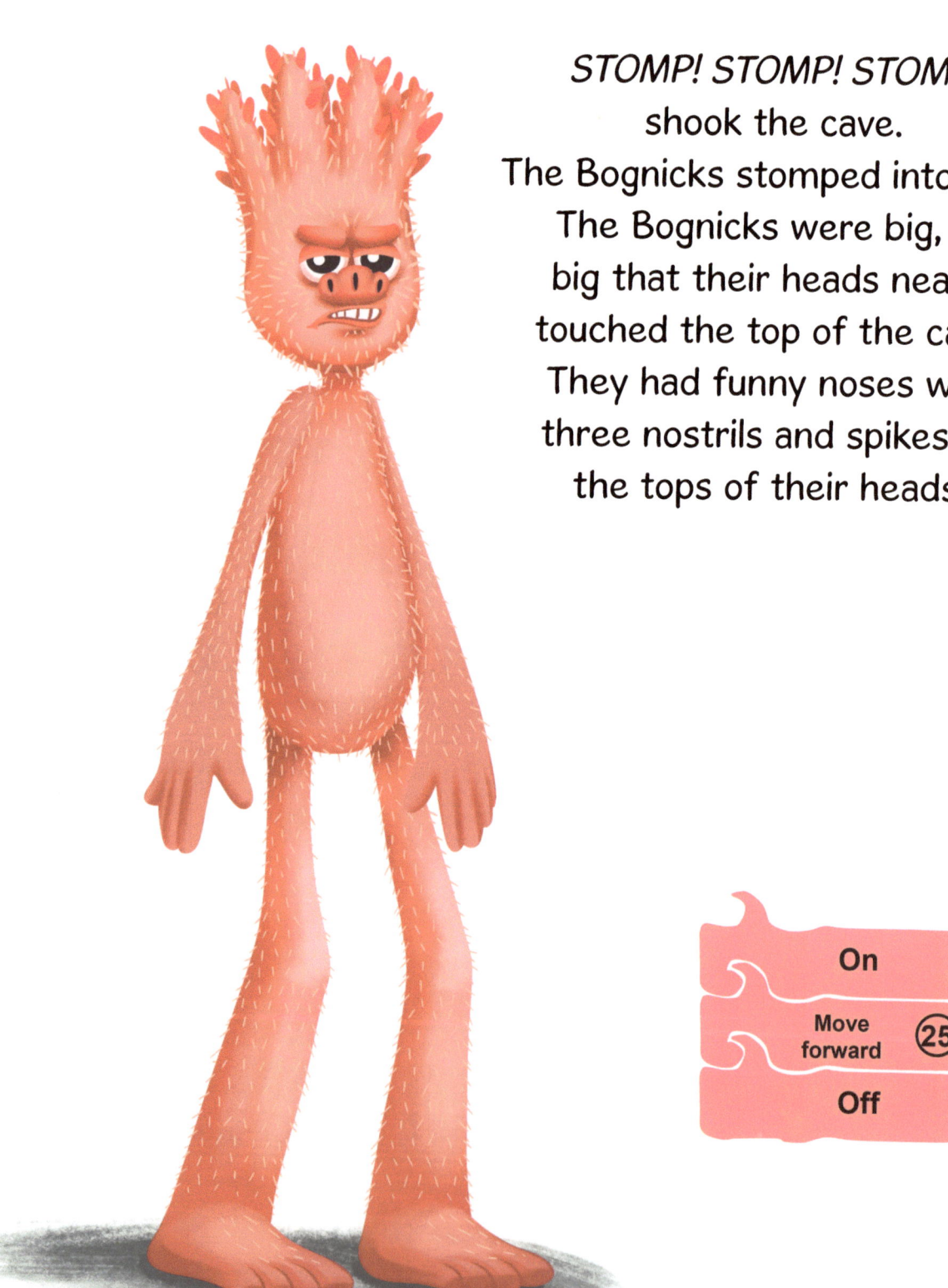

STOMP! STOMP! STOMP!
shook the cave.
The Bognicks stomped into view.
The Bognicks were big, so
big that their heads nearly
touched the top of the cave.
They had funny noses with
three nostrils and spikes on
the tops of their heads.

On
Move forward (25)
Off

EXPERIENCE THIS IN AR

SCAN QR CODE › POINT PHONE AT PAGE › DISCOVER EXPERIENCE

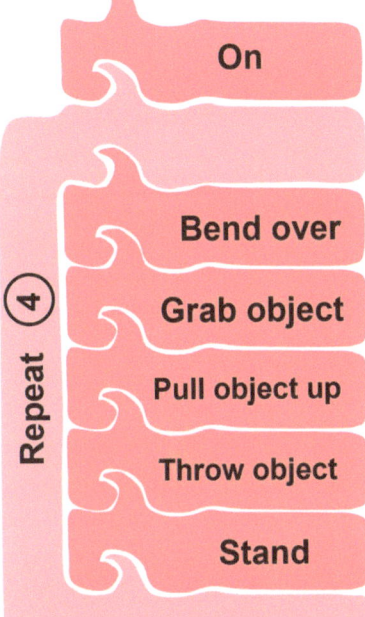

On
Repeat 4
Bend over
Grab object
Pull object up
Throw object
Stand
Off

The Bognicks bent down and
began to pull the plants with
glowing leaves from the sand.
'No!' cried the Trix Kix.
'Stop!' cried the Ick Erros.
'Don't do that!' cried
Zoom and Stephen.
But their cries did not work.
The Bognicks pulled *more*
plants from the sand.

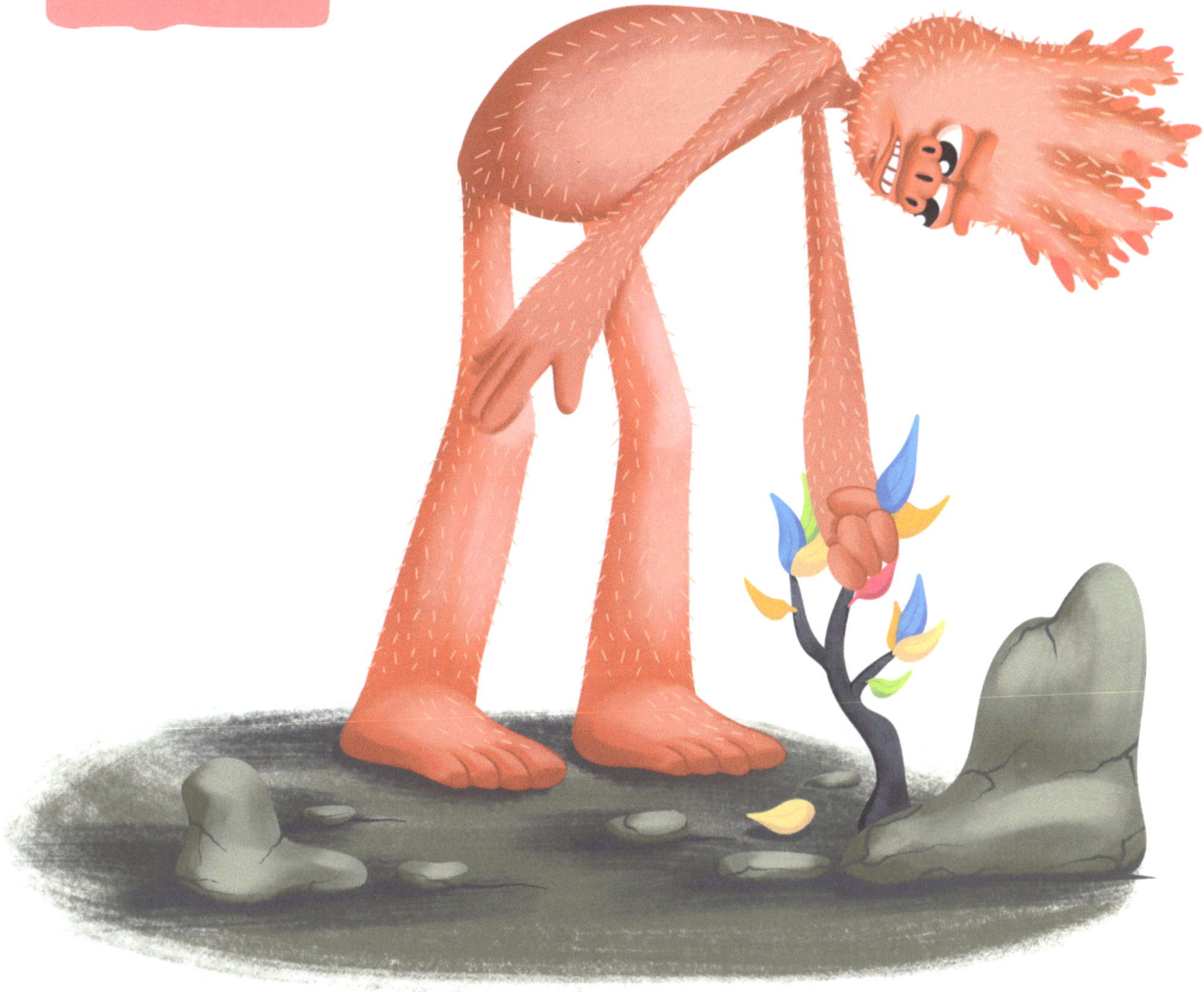

EXPERIENCE THIS IN AR

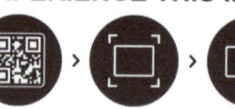

'Get lost, you nasty beasts!'
shouted the Ick Erros.
'Go away, you dumb drongos!'
shouted the Trix Kix.
'Shoo, you silly galahs!' shouted
Zoom and Stephen.
But their shouts did not work.
The Bognicks pulled *more*
plants out of the sand.

The Trix Kix marched to the Bognicks
and stomped on their big hairy feet.
The Bognicks ignored the Trix Kix.

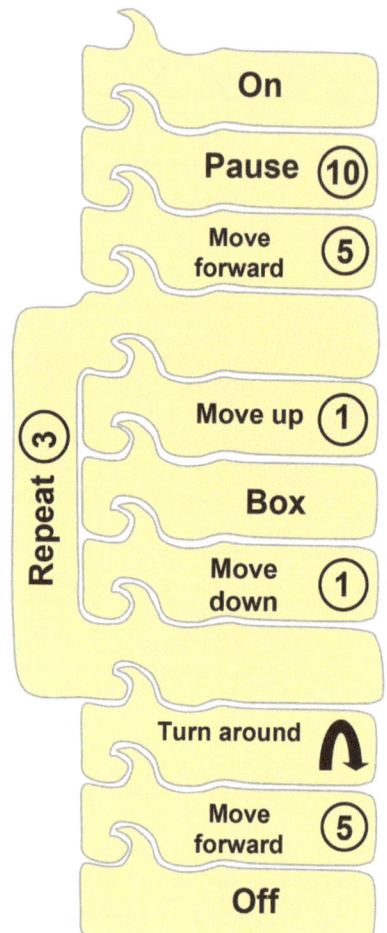

The Ick Erros leapt up high to box the
Bognicks on their big hairy chests.
The Bognicks ignored the Ick Erros.
Zoom and Stephen flapped their wings
and squawked at the Bognicks.
The Bognicks ignored Zoom and Stephen.
The Bognicks pulled *more* plants out of the sand.

On

Repeat 5
- Bend over
- Grab object
- Pull object up
- Throw object
- Stand

Off

'We challenge you to a shell-throwing contest!
If we win, you must go,' called the Trix Kix.
'If we lose, you can stay,' called the Ick Erros.
The Bognicks stopped pulling plants out of the sand.
Grunt! Grumble! Gurgle!
The Bognicks made funny noises and they nodded.

The Trix Kix, the Ick Erros, Zoom, Stephen and the Bognicks each found a perfect shell. Zoom's shell had brown spots, and Stephen's shell was the colour of the sunset.
It was time for the shell-throwing contest to begin.

The Trix Kix would throw first.
They held their shells high in their legs, ready to throw.
'Cavoy, Cavah, Cavoo!' shouted the Trix Kix
as they threw with all their might.
The shells thrown by the little Trix Kix went
as far as they could throw them.
Ha! Ha! Ha! the Bognicks laughed.
They did not think that the Trix Kix had thrown very far.

The Ick Erros would throw second.
They held their shells high in their
webbed hands, ready to throw.
'Cavoy, Cavah, Cavoo!' shouted the Ick Erros
as they threw with all their might.
The shells thrown by the medium-
sized Ick Erros went farther.
Ha! Ha! Ha! the Bognicks laughed again.
They did not think that the Ick Erros had thrown very far.

The Bognicks would throw third.
They held their shells high in their big
hairy hands, ready to throw.
'Cavoy, Cavah, Cavoo!' shouted the Bognicks
as they threw with all their might.
The shells thrown by the big Bognicks went even farther.
Poof! Poof! Poof!
The Bognicks puffed up like pigeons.

Zoom and Stephen would throw fourth.
The Trix Kix and the Ick Erros trembled with worry.
Zoom and Stephen shook with fear.
Stephen asked, 'Do you think we can win the contest?'
Zoom paused to think about the problem.

As Zoom thought, an orange glowing leaf blew past.
Zoom watched the leaf blow by.
'Stephen, we'll throw in the opposite direction,' Zoom whispered.
Stephen paused and thought about what Zoom had whispered.
A blue glowing leaf blew past.
Stephen understood and winked at Zoom.

Zoom and Stephen turned to face the opposite direction.
The Trix Kix, the Ick Erros and the Bognicks stared.
They wondered what the two strange birds were doing.
Why were Zoom and Stephen throwing in the opposite direction?

Zoom and Stephen held their shells
high in their wings, ready to throw.
'Cavoy, Cavah, Cavoo!' shouted
Zoom and Stephen as they
threw with all their might.
The shells thrown by Zoom
and Stephen went very far.
This time the Bognicks did not laugh.
Everyone looked at each
other, their eyes wide.
Who had won the contest?
'We will measure!' said the Trix Kix.

- On
- Raise object
- Say [Cavoy, Cavah, Cavoo!]
- Throw object
- Pause (10)
- Shrug
- Pause (5)
- Nod
- Off

- On
- Raise object
- Say "Cavoy, Cavah, Cavoo!"
- Throw object
- Pause 10
- Shrug
- Pause 5
- Nod
- Off

EXPERIENCE THIS IN AR

 SCAN QR CODE >  POINT PHONE AT PAGE >  DISCOVER EXPERIENCE

The Ick Erros lay down in the
sand, one by one, with their feet
touching the head of another.
First, they measured how far the shells
thrown by the Trix Kix had gone.
Their shells had travelled
six Ick Erros away!
'Ooh!' everyone said.
Next, they measured how far the shells
thrown by the Ick Erros had gone.
Their shells had travelled
ten Ick Erros away!
'Aah!' everyone said.

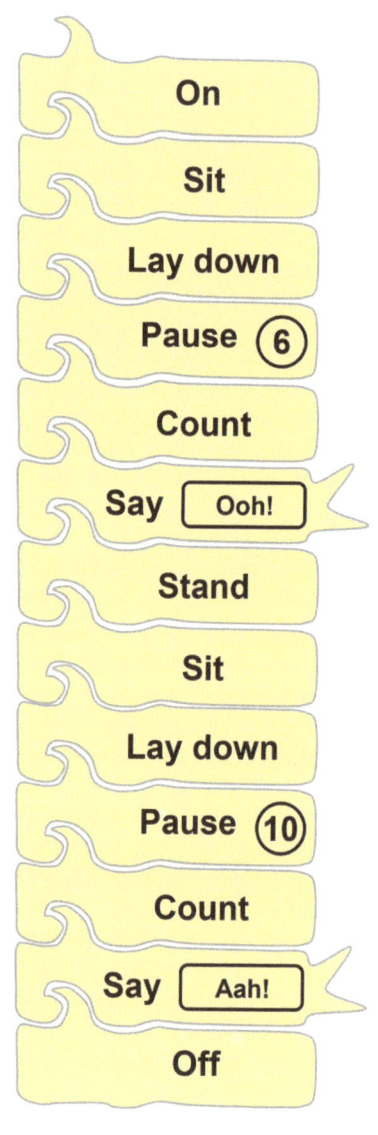

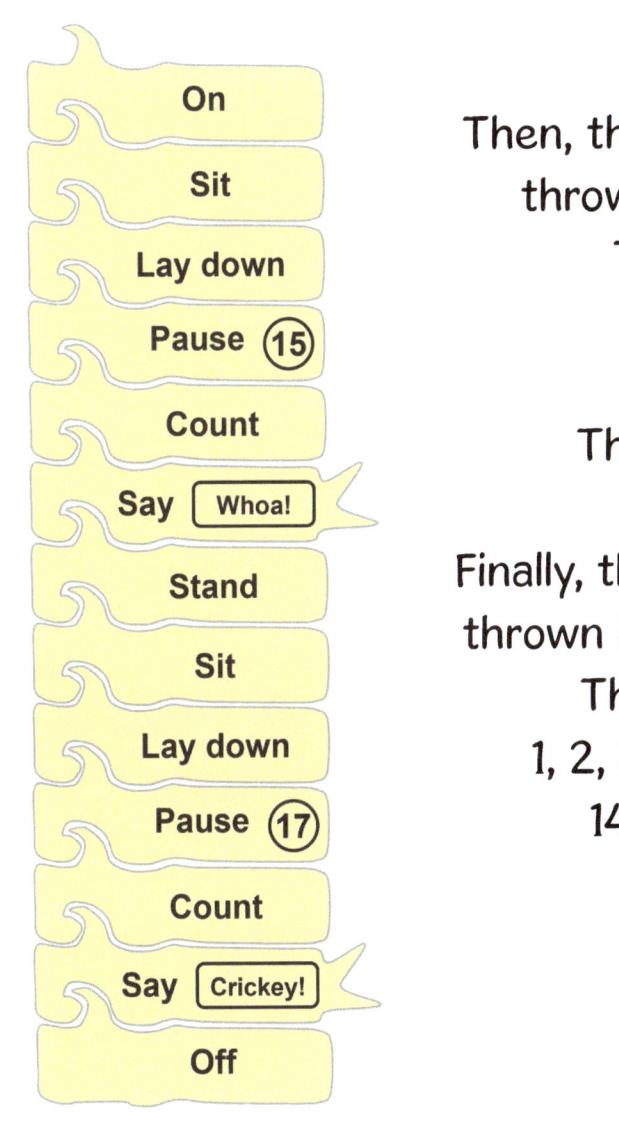

Then, they measured how far the shells thrown by the Bognicks had gone. Their shells had travelled fifteen Ick Erros away! 'Whoa!' everyone said. The Ick Erros hopped over in the opposite direction. Finally, they measured how far the shells thrown by Zoom and Stephen had gone. Their shells had travelled . . . 1, 2, 3, 4, 5, 6, 7, 8, 9, 10, 11, 12, 13, 14, 15, 16, 17 Ick Erros away! 'Crickey!' everyone said.

The Trix Kix and the Ick Erros gathered around Zoom and Stephen and cheered. The shells thrown by Zoom and Stephen had gone the farthest! Zoom and Stephen had solved the problem. They had thrown in the direction the wind was blowing. The wind helped their shells travel farther!

Zoom and Stephen had won the shell-throwing contest! *Grunt! Grumble! Groan!* The Bognicks made funny noises and they shook their heads. Then the Bognicks turned and walked away. *CRUNCH! CRUNCH! CRUNCH!* went the shells under their feet.

Zoom and Stephen helped to replant the pulled-out plants. The leaves of the plants glowed and twinkled again, as if winking at Zoom and Stephen.

Zoom and Stephen were tired — it was time to go home.
Zoom and Stephen went into a dark tunnel.
Inside the tunnel, a wind gust pushed Zoom and Stephen up, up, up.
Whoosh! Swoosh! went the wind blowing through their feathers.

One mighty *whoosh* more,
Zoom and Stephen rocketed out from beneath the reef.
They landed on their feathery behinds
back on the soft white sand.

Zoom turned to Stephen and said, 'I reckon
we should dig another hole tomorrow.'
Stephen answered, 'Bonza idea, mate!'

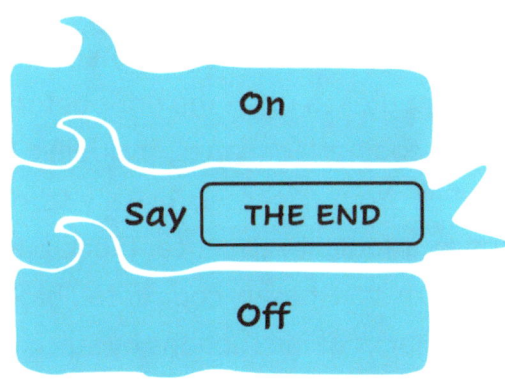

What is coding?

Coding is a list of step-by-step instructions, like a recipe, that gets computers to do what you want them to do. These step-by-step instructions are also called algorithms.

Computer algorithms are written in a logical order so that computers can complete the tasks. Computers are machines which cannot think the way that living things with brains can think. Instead, computers are coded to follow very specific instructions. A computer will only do what it is programmed to do if those instructions are in a logical order. For example, if a computer is programmed to enter a room with a door, the program must instruct the computer to open the door before walking into the room.

There are many text-based coding languages, including Python, JavaScript, Java, C#, C, C++, R, Go, Swift and PHP. Young learners usually start coding by using blocks of code to represent steps in a logical sequence. Block-based coding is a process where software developers turn text-based code into "blocks" of instructions that can be sequenced into larger blocks of instructions by stacking the blocks in a logical order. With block coding, young people can learn foundational concepts through simple visuals instead of needing to know how to write text-based code. Block coding software platforms such as Scratch, Snap and Blockly are often used to create animated games, characters and stories.

A person using and writing computer code is called a coder.

How is coding used in *Cavoy, Cavah, Cavoo!*?

A representation of code blocks is used to symbolise the actions of the characters in *Cavoy, Cavah, Cavoo!* to make foundational coding concepts accessible to early readers. Representing the characters' actions in text and illustrations, like a typical picture book, and in a visual representation of block code, teaches readers how code is related to a sequence of actions in a story. The combination of text, illustrations and code blocks will foster a reader's ability to understand logic and algorithms similar to the instructions that are written to program computers.

Why is it important to learn code?

As humanity progresses through the 21st century, coding has become an increasingly important skill and part of our lives. Coding is already all around us, in smartphones, tablets, smart TVs, automated cars, traffic lights and automated check-out machines in the supermarkets, to name a few.

Learning to code is a fundamental skill which will be as important as learning to read. Coders use logic to design and program computer software and applications (apps). Beyond being able to program computers and write computer software, coders have skills in breaking down problems into manageable chunks. Coders do more than consume digital media and instead are the creators of new software, including websites, apps and system software, to solve current and future global problems.

What is Augmented Reality (AR)?

Augmented Reality (AR) lets us see the real-life environment with a digital augmentation overlaid on it. In *Cavoy, Cavah, Cavoo!*, the characters are animated with movement and sound when a smartphone (or other similar smart device) with an Internet connection is used to interact with the QR codes in the book.

AR is used in *Cavoy, Cavah, Cavoo!* to help readers to learn how the code relates to the characters' actions and to provide a more exciting and immersive reading experience. Young people will delight in seeing the characters 'come to life', taking them beyond the realms of a typical picture book. Readers can also relate the visual movement depicted in the AR experience directly to the code as the code blocks light up in when the actions are being performed.

How to read *Cavoy, Cavah, Cavoo!*

Cavoy, Cavah, Cavoo! can be read like a typical picture book. If the reader does not have a smartphone or smart device with an Internet connection, the reader will be able to experience the adventures of Zoom and Stephen and their new friends beneath the reef through the text, the illustrations and the code block representations. The experience will be similar to reading a typical picture book, with the addition of illustrated representations of code blocks which break the characters' actions into sets of steps. The code blocks mimic the happenings of the book and can help readers improve their digital literacy as they engage in language and literacy.

How to use Augmented Reality (AR) in *Cavoy, Cavah, Cavoo!*

If the reader has access to a smartphone, or other similar smart device, and an Internet connection, the reader can animate the illustrations that are accompanied by QR codes. To activate the AR experiences, the reader will hold their smart device over the QR code. The reader will need to use the camera app or a QR code reader app to scan the QR code. The QR code will take the reader to a website which has a 'Launch' button. The reader will need to 'Grant Access' to their device's camera and motion sensors. Once access has been granted, the reader holds their device over the illustration on the same page that has the QR code. The AR experience will load, animating the characters and illuminating the code blocks which represent the characters' actions.

To load a new AR experience, the reader navigates back to the camera app or QR code reader to scan the new QR code that matches the new illustration. The reader repeats the process described previously. The AR experiences will consolidate the reader's foundational understanding of how blocks of code are used to represent a sequence of simple steps.